Carcharias taurus

Dr. Jaws

Carcharias taurus
Copyright © 2013 by Zachary Webb Nicholls

All rights reserved. Published in the United States by Deep Sea Publishing LLC, Herndon, Virginia.

ISBN-13: 978-1-939535-10-8
ISBN: 1939535107
E-Book ISBN-13: 978-1-939535-15-3
E-Book ISBN: 1939535158

www.deepseapublishing.com

Printed in the United States of America

Hello friend,

What you are about to read is secret.

Each word, picture, and symbol has a meaning, and together they will help you find something very strange, but very exciting. Furthermore, each word, picture, and symbol is anchored in a living truth, but in order to fully understand what that truth is, you need to do some exploring.

Beyond this little book, there is a boundless, bountiful wealth of knowledge within your reach. You of course are not required to seek it, but if you do, I assure you will be rewarded with a richer understanding of our shark, the seas, and the mystery of life itself.

For now, you hold in your hands a map. Let it take you—from the past, to the present, to the weird—deep into an ocean of legends, of dark wonders, and of amber eyes…

….let it take you to Shark.

Carcharias taurus

The Curse of Edward Teach

Dr. Jaws

What he brought with Roanoke

Could not have been replaced

And when he took his twenty cuts

We thought his death embraced

But little did we understand

When Anne sank into sea

That down there in the shadows

Pirate Teach still may be...

Starlight is finite
A star has a time to end
Explosive its death

Scattered star pieces
Combine into the combined
Birth of sun and earth

Sun fire creates
With calm earth, air, and water
Life elemental

~ *Domain Eukarya* ~

Imagine a mountain

Cool and calming

Trickling water down its slope

It is serene in its grey

Paint it with a domain

Of life so rich in color

That the eyes will forever wonder

At its design and sustain

A curiosity

Unique only to Eukarya

When cell within cell became cell itself

So long ago, a peak

In life was reached

From origins so humble

Came oranges so fiery

With jades, emeralds, and harlequins each

Beauties of the forest

Protecting the ambling reds

And boisterous blues

With calming arms best

Suited for shading

Amber-centered violets

And cinnabar-sighted mosaics

All art never fading

This domain is of color

See Eukarya

Splendid and diverse

Muses of the world

For the art that it is

~*Kingdom Animalia*~

Look what the dawn has broken

Something new stirs in the seas

A novel language now spoken

The animals have come to be

~

From one tiny sponge to one funny man

A simple life will always be banned

A drama that we cannot understand

The animals, come and play, come and
play

A hardworking ant meets an unfriendly beetle

While two birds romance, it seems nothing's sweeter

A seahorse's dance is such a unique love

Animals, come and play, come and play

~

Embrace the feeling of life

A body that's one from many

A hunger that sets you right

~

And chase in manner uncanny

Your strange sweet compassions

You animal, go and play, go and play

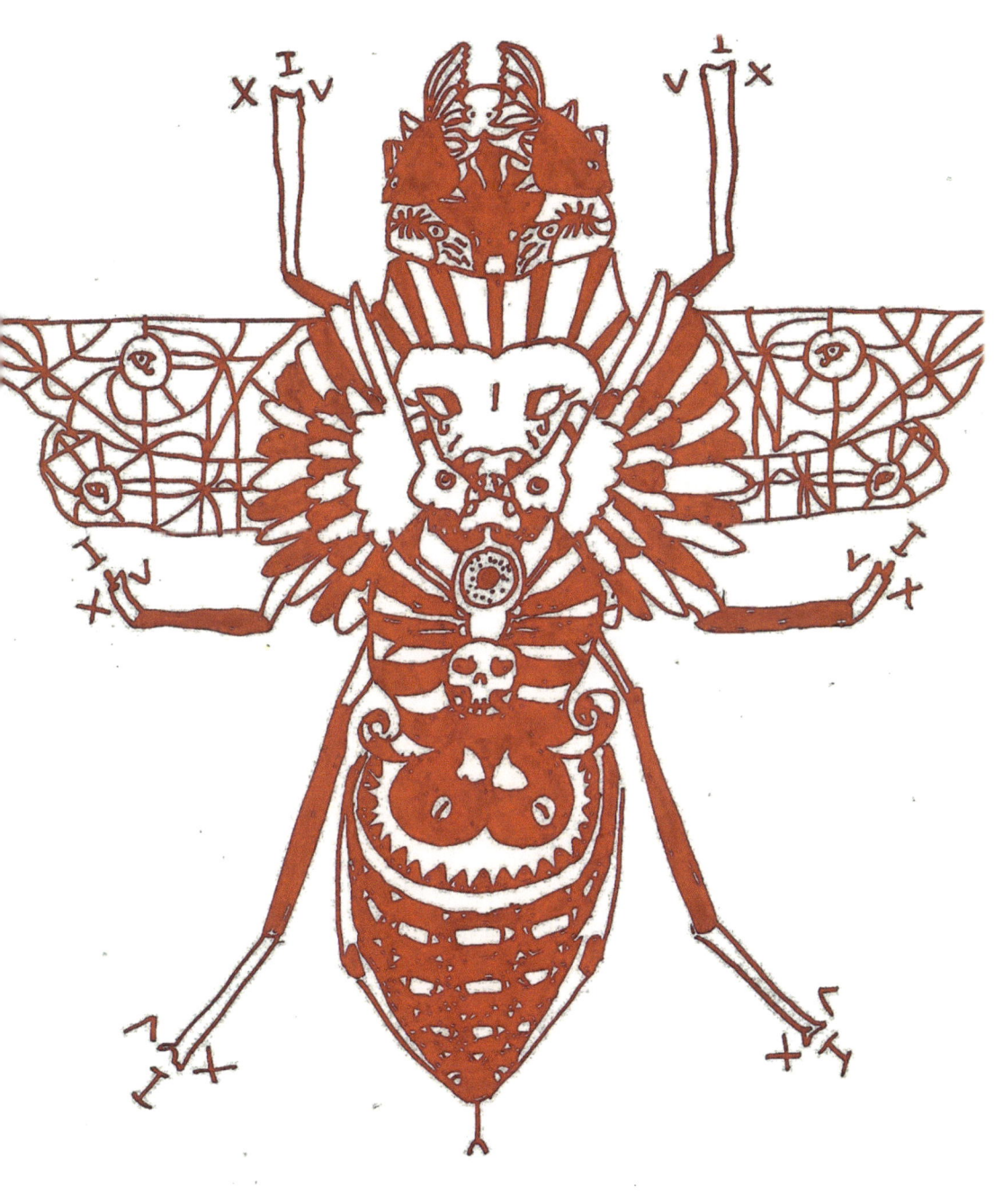

~Phylum Chordata~

~ *Class Chondrichthyes* ~

There is a hall of marble and limestone—of honor and ocean—adorned with obsidian shadows; the Chondrichthyan Silhouettes. Each Silhouette is an embodiment of form and essence, said to be constructed by the gods to remind the world of the Living Shadows; the chimaera, the ray, and the shark.

Believed to be guardians of both the ocean and the human soul, The Living Shadows served to consume the weaknesses of each. Through so doing, they culled corruption and protected the life of both soul and sea.

To honor this nobility cloaked in ferocity, the Chondrichthyan Silhouettes are each adorned with an eye of pearl and gemstone. Together, body and eye capture the essence of a Living Shadow:

A power cooled with grace

An immortal who could die

A legend with a heartbeat.

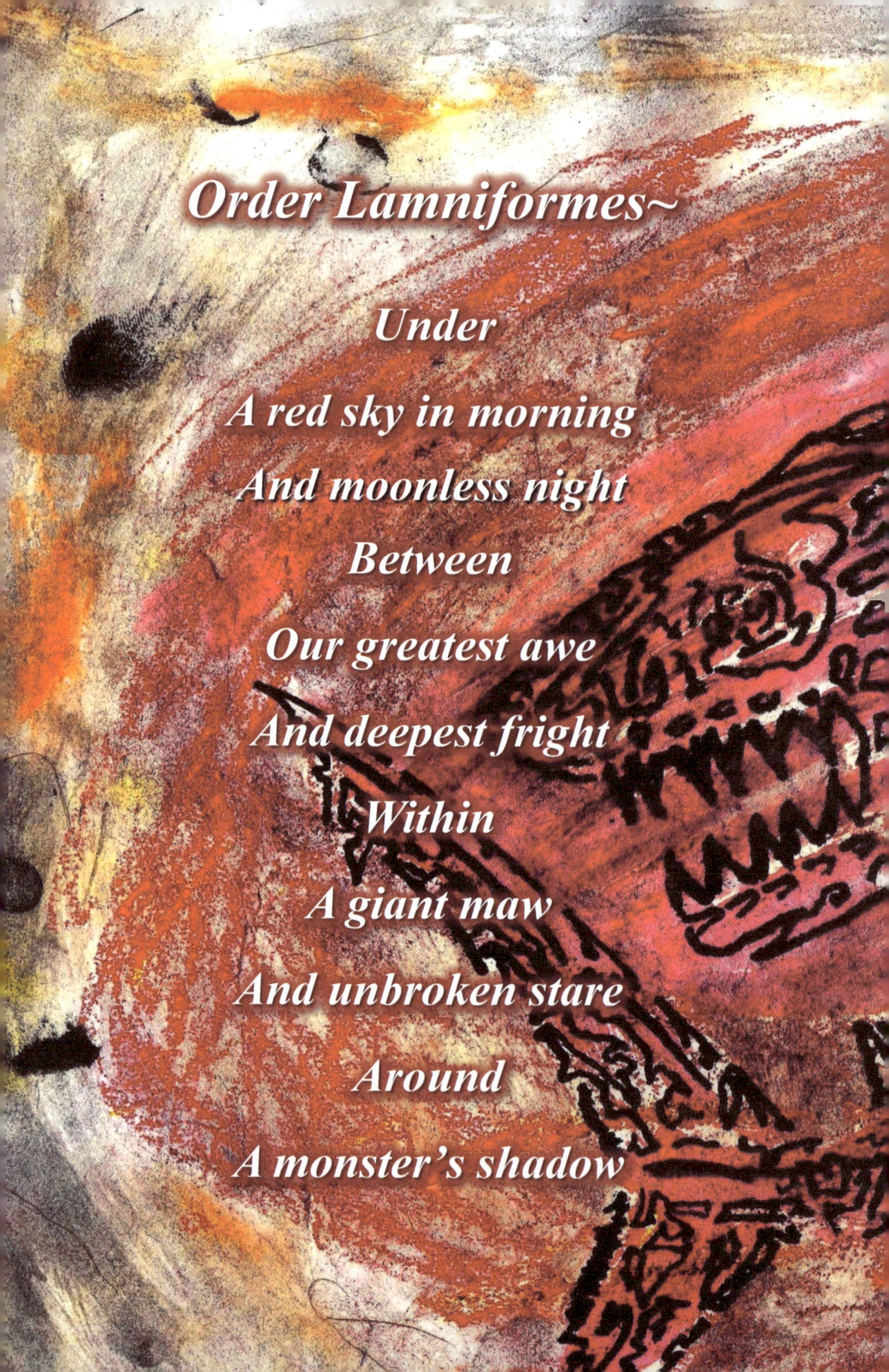

Order Lamniformes~

Under

A red sky in morning

And moonless night

Between

Our greatest awe

And deepest fright

Within

A giant maw

And unbroken stare

Around

A monster's shadow

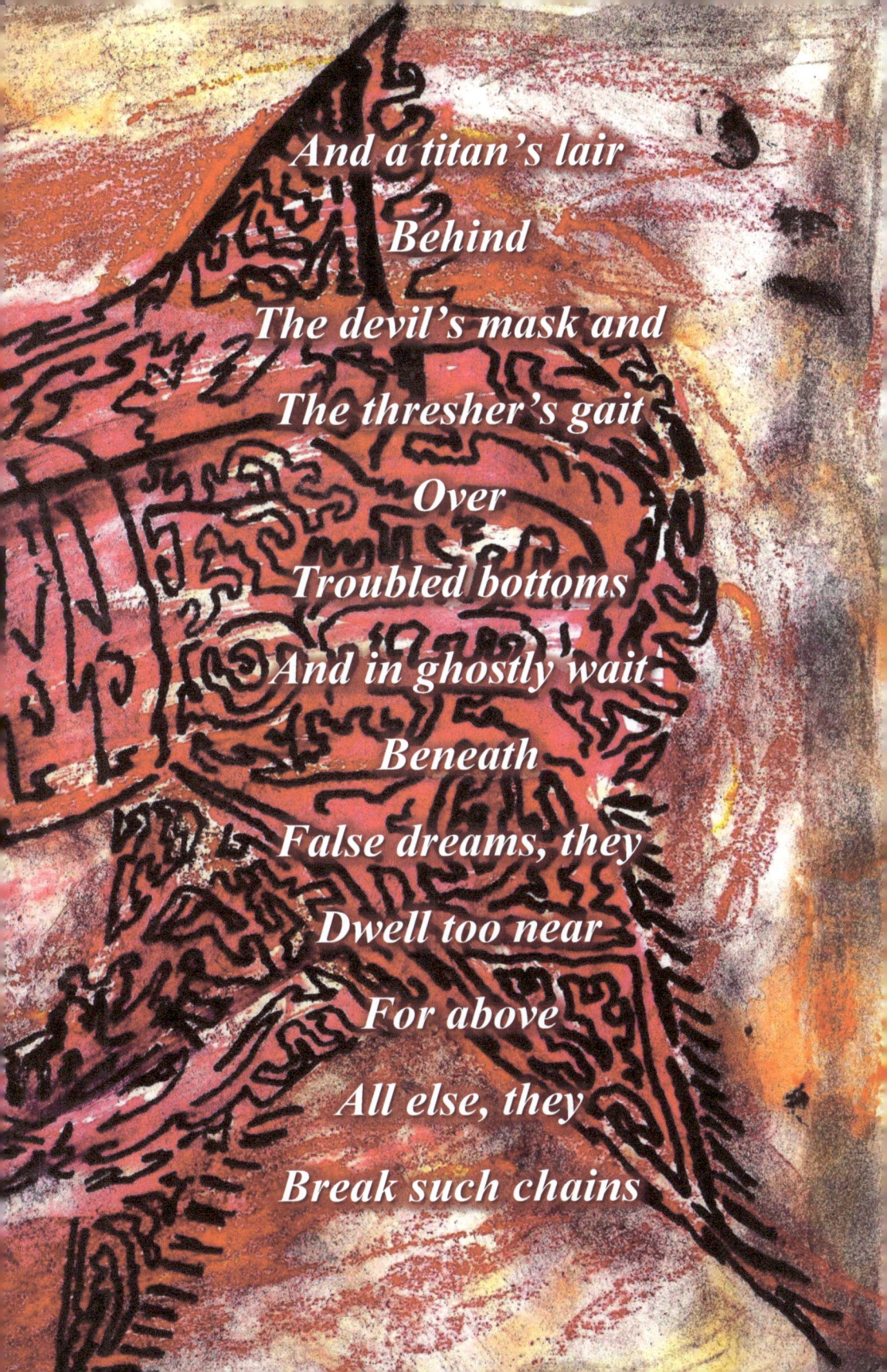

And a titan's lair

Behind

The devil's mask and

The thresher's gait

Over

Troubled bottoms

And in ghostly wait

Beneath

False dreams, they

Dwell too near

For above

All else, they

Break such chains

~Family Odontaspididae~

The sandtiger sharks

Lurkers of the serpent's tooth

Fangs be always bared

~*Genus Carcharias*~

SHARK

"Pquo oqrmc'o enrmojg rkknrmrhfn, "ocuh je fjuhrsn", rhi edjwuhs euho mnguhuofnhp je r qnrvy fjrp uhokumni hjpquhs ndon atp r Adrfcanrmi opjmy uh gy guhi"

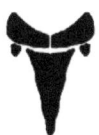

Note: The above is a keyword cypher. The keyword is hidden on the following page. Use it to unlock a smaller insight.

The Bull

Carcharias taurus

Rafinesque, 1810

Carcharias taurus

A medium-sized shark, with an average mass of 100kg. It is unmistakable with its protruding teeth, conical snout, and equally sized dorsal fins.

Sandtiger   Tiburón toro

ریت چیتا شارک   錐齒鯊   シロワニ

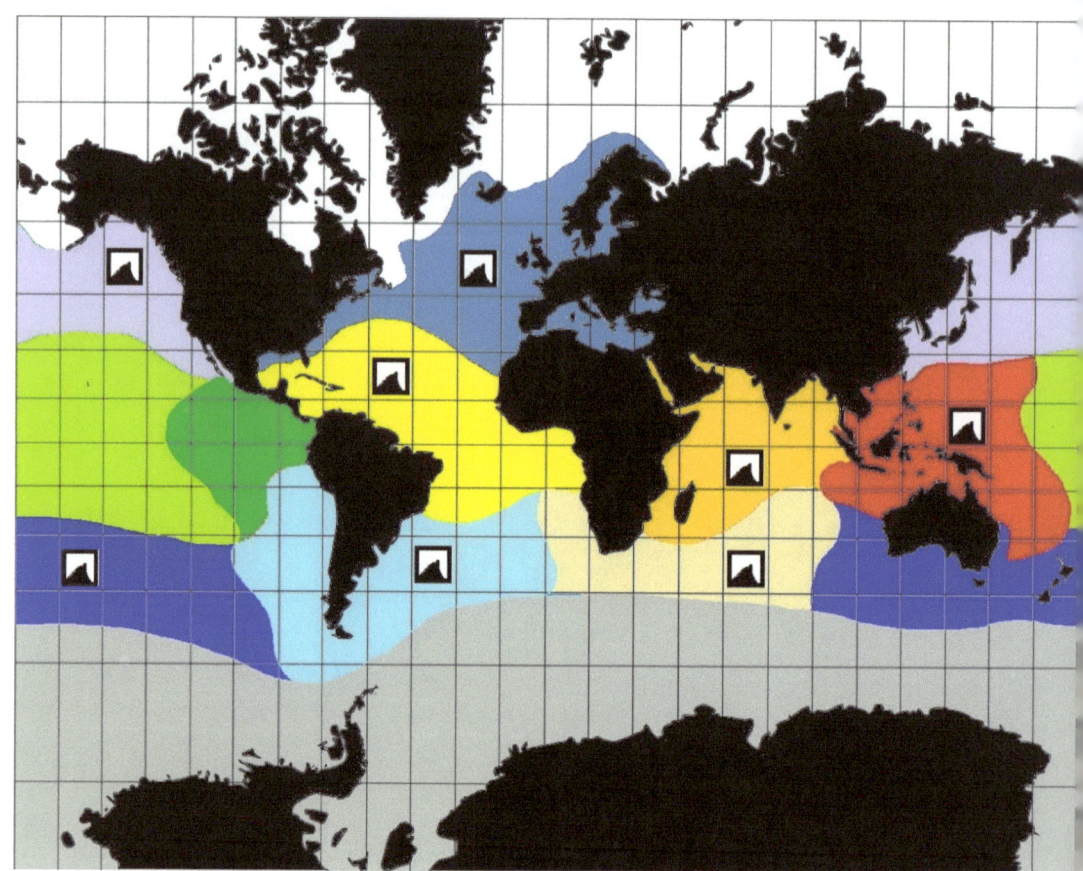

~*Global Distribution*~

North Akula Sea

Tempest Requin Sea

Wild Zame Sea

Sunset Sea of Reken

Colorful Sea of Sarka

Bountiful Sea of Shayu

Peaceful Sea of Mano

Sunrise Sea of Tiburon

Grande Tubarao Sea

Groot Haai Sea

Great Shark Sea

South Sarko Sea

~Haunts~

Carcharias taurus

can be found in the following zones:

Littoral

Neritic

Sunlit

and the following special habitats:

Coral Reefs

"This dome to which we hath been bound poureth riches beyond admiration into our most receiving mouths. Though the sea hath claimeth her once-glorious mien, the ship retaineth her essence of plenty as evident by the presence of fish specious to both the eye and belly. With such quiet as this, none would hath suspecteth that we beest of a devoted crew."

~ *Habits* ~

Carcharias taurus is famed for its particularly lurid reproductive strategy of intrauterine cannibalism. Within the mother's 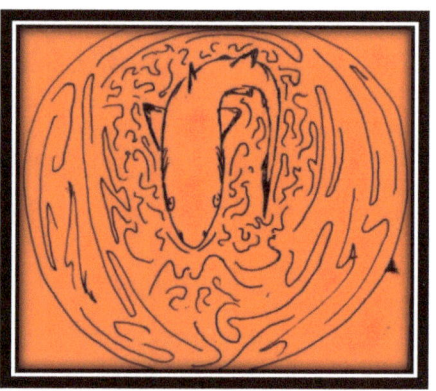 womb, the two strongest developing pups will devour their siblings. In spite of this gruesome beginning, *Carcharias taurus* is typically docile in nature. The species is an unchoosy consumer of fish and invertebrates. It enjoys spending time near reefs, caves, and shipwrecks.

Uniquely, *Carcharias taurus* can swallow air to maintain neutral buoyancy; this ability allows it to hover motionless underwater.

~ *Humanity* ~

Carcharias taurus is to be perceived as a

POTENTIALLY DANGEROUS SHARK

In light of the concerning attributes that follow;

Its fearsome dentition

Its considerable size

Its proximity to man

These attributes are juxtaposed with the truth that

Carcharias taurus has been implicated in

RELATIVELY FEW UNPROVOKED ATTACKS

As a resource, the shark offers palatable meat, and is a popular focus of ecotourism and public aquaria.

~

However, man has overfished Carcharias taurus, subjected the shark to the cruelty of finning, and furthermore strangled individuals through the implementation of beach meshing.

As a result, Carcharias taurus is a

VULNERABLE SPECIES

~The Curse of Edward Teach ~

"A tale about our shark, and more…"

John Smith was an ambitious man...

Much like his namesake, he was adventurous, daring, and passionately intrusive of the far corners of the world; he was in Cuba when Castro first came to power, China when Mao conducted his Cultural Revolution, and Alaska where Smith himself became forcibly detained for his suspected promotion of the communist ideal. Ironically, Smith's agenda on these misadventures was far from the school of spreading wealth, but rather in the ambition of keeping it for himself.

He was a treasure hunter, and a good one at that. It was Smith who salvaged the first doubloons of the Havana 400, the first jades of Xiuqiushan's tomb...even in Alaska, before his arrest, Smith was on the trail of pirate gold on the Islands of Adak. Of course, he reported to his captors that he was in The Last Frontier for the fishing, and that his potentially red associations from journeys past were nothing more than subjects of his own cultural interest. This lie was sufficient, as the educated John Smith was sincerely passionate about both history and travel. However, it was all too necessary; the priceless pieces that he acquired from his skill were sold on the black market, and for highest reasonable price.

His newest quarry, however, was far closer to home as the daring explorer did not wish to attract any more unwanted attention. Smith was especially anxious in regards to this particular expedition, as it concerned a wreck of untold riches and insurmountable notoriety: The *Queen Anne's Revenge*, flagship of the most infamous Edward Teach.

Guided by a map of antiquity and a crew of unambiguity, Smith journey's forth to the Beaufort Inlet…on a turbid summer day in 1972…

"You've outdone yourself this time, John!" shouted Evans (Smith's North Carolina contact) over the sound's choppy waves, "You're absolutely positive that this is Spotswood's map?"

"Yes", began the cocksure Smith, "you can find both his AND Robert Maynard's signature on the back. But look at the front right here, near the shoreline…those symbols aren't Western; the closest thing I can compare it to is Mattaponi, but it has peculiarities…"

"That's wild", replied his friend. Smiling, he added, "and what do you make of this 'X' off of Beaufort?"

"That's got to be where he scuttled her", assured Smith. "I bought this map from a woman named Christina Rae, a self-proclaimed descendant of Governor Alexander Spotswood. According to her, Maynard collected both this and the letter to Justice Tobias Knight off of Teach's person…after the duel of course…the

Judge's letter has been historically verified, but this map has never been mentioned…"

"It might make sense though", proffered Evans, "Spotswood wouldn't have wanted this map to be publicly known if—"

"—if he thought the 'X' marked treasure." Smith concluded. "It might not be what he was thinking, but *Queen Anne's Revenge* as a wreck will still fetch a high price, whether we find pieces of eight or wooden spoons!"

At hearing this, the third member of their crew piped up with alarm, "Y'all never told me you'd be messin' with Blackbeard's wreck". He started to steer away from Beaufort Inlet. "Them waters be haunted out the wazoo… dangerous place to be pokin' around…"

"It's alright, skipper!" called an amused Smith. "Teach died much further north on the *Adventure*. If he has a restless spirit, it'll be stuck in Ocracoke."

"Y'all don't understand." continued the dissuaded fisherman; he was hired for his superior local knowledge of these waters, but kept in the dark of the mission's true purpose. "At night—especially a night with no moon—you can see them Teach's Lights all-a-buzzing off of the waves. Some say you can even see the devil's headless body lurkin' if you be pokin' around too long…"

"Stay on course, skipper," spoke a firmer Evans, who was expecting a share of whatever profit may come, "I'm not so much concerned about ghosts as I am about the water." He was eyeing the increasing chop and far distant thunder. Though the fiery Carolina sun was now passionately kissing the slate-blue strength of The Graveyard's waters, the impeding clouds threatened drama enough to shatter the intimacy.

"This might not be the best day to do it, John…" began a disheartened Evans.

"No, I think it's the perfect day," Smith dismissed. "A little rough water just enhances the thrill!"

"But," continued the concerned accomplice, "you're going at it alone. Even on a good day that's flawed thinking."

"Well fine, then I picked a crap day," muttered Smith nonchalantly as he assembled his gear. They were nearing their destination. "It's happened before, it'll happen again."

Evans did not continue. They reached the inlet.

"Head towards the sun a little, skipper...the ship would have moved after two-centuries and a half." Smith calculated the proper location beforehand, considering the tides and what history he could ascertain about Beaufort's currents. When they reached the only spot that would satisfy him, the fully-suited Smith hopped over the port side and slid calmly in the water. Evans secured his diving line and deployed the telltale red flag. He then handed Smith a light, his dive knife, and a collecting bag.

"Be careful," said Evans with earnest eyes. He was starting to feel dread.

"If Coast Guard shows, tell them I'm on an oyster reef. I'll be back in an hour."

And with that, John Smith began his descent.

Lapping
Blue
Empty
Down
Shimmer
School
Bluefish
Distant
Shadow
Looming
Sand
Mound
Manmade
Ship
Wood
Encrusted
Intact
Sharks

Smith was dead-accurate as to his chosen location, for before him lay an extensive mass of wood, sand, and sealife. Partially claimed by the seafloor, *Queen Anne's Revenge* looked no-less magnificent, as little ghosts of surface light played amongst her encrusted timbers, darting through tiny meadows of algae and anemones on a handsome wooden base. Smith, however, was not alone…a shiver of Sandtigers was around him.

Big, scary, but subtly coated with a golden sheen, they were the perfect compliments to this wreck. Another man may have died of fright—about 13 were around the site—but Smith well understood the sharks' true nature. These were beasts of a calmer sort, innocuous and unobtrusive. Some may be curious, yes, but they mostly kept to themselves…after all, they were just as wary of the diver's hulking mass and noisy bubbles as Smith was of their unbreakable gaze and pointy teeth.

He began to explore. He apparently was at the stern and was approaching slowly on the mainsail. To his delight, he spied an open hatch to what lay below, but he continued bow-ward with hopes of coming back later. *Queen Anne's* current horizon was a heavy clash of deep blue and sandy white. Large black boulders brought relief to the emptiness and played host to an amazing variety of coolwater fish and invertebrates; Black Sea Bass frolicked with some baby spadefish, Tautog were gracefully darting in and out of whatever crevices they could find, and gigantic Cobia patrolled the tops of the mounds as if they were the lords of this haunt.

As pleasant as this layout was to behold, the bow held no secrets, and Smith returned to the spot which he felt most likely concealed something of value. But as he made this second approach, he noticed that the Sandtigers changed their behavior. Ever so slightly, they quickened their pace, and swam in a more orderly fashion…

Perhaps they *wanted* him to go down the hatch…

Smith mistakenly took this as a good omen. Diving alone is a folly in itself, but diving alone AND within a structure of unknown stability was pure idiocy. Nonetheless, John Smith's desire for wealth commanded him to forgo all precaution and see for himself what riches lay below.

Down the hatch he went.

Blue water became his ceiling, while ordered oaken shadows created the halls and walls of curiosity. Before him lay a passage to what he believed to be the captain's quarters, while around him were promising signs of treasures to come: as he progressed, he passed two pairs of gambling dice, one jaw-harp barely visible in the overgrowth, and—to his great excitement—a pipe-piece that looked as though it were made of ivory. Smith had to see what was behind the door at the end, for it was only slightly ajar and seemed to conceal a secret…for sure, something of Blackbeard's must be within this chamber…

He opened it.

He regretted his decision.

John Smith was staring down an enormous Sandtiger heavily scarred and absolutely still. Its presence alone made the diver jump…but now, as he settled from the initial shock, a far more insidious feeling was creeping in. There was something very wrong with this room…with this animal…Smith couldn't place it, but this scene was…intended…

The Sandtiger was watching him, its eyes fixed through the mask and into Smith's soul. The diver needed to leave. Smith backpedaled towards the door, keeping his eyes on the bristled maw. His progress, however, came to an immediate halt when he heard the disembodied voice:

"Tellest me of the bedlam from which thou surely emergest…for thou art of serious distemper to be so bold as to disturb me…"

The room immediately changed.

Somehow, Smith found himself dry, standing, and in period clothing; he was breathing the air of a stuffy room, and beheld a proper captain's quarters with fresh furnishings. Sunlight was pouring in, and out of the corner of his eye he could see from repaired windows a warm harbor that housed a plethora of old clipper ships. His primary gaze was still fixed on where the shark was, but the beast had been replaced.

A man now stood before him. He was tall and seemed rather thin, but it was hard to tell as he was wearing an enormous dark overcoat. He had knee-length black boots and a wide black tricorn, but both were contrasted with a blood-red vest. The man's most distinguishing feature was however his beard. It was long, dirty, and mangled black, with red silk ribbons trying to tame it into pigtails. There was no doubt as to who he was.

"Blackbeard?" mumbled a bewildered Smith.

The man made no reply. He just stared. Smith's uneasiness was rapidly increasing. He felt as if he were obliged to say something, but he could not possibly know what. The unbearable silence persisted. The man then walked to his right and broke his gaze in favor of attending to the captain's chair. He waived his hand gracefully towards a seat opposite, and Smith obeyed. A table was between them.

In a calm, practiced, but icy English voice, the man began, "State thy business and reason for such impertinence."

Though Smith was still baffled by his present situation, he automatically replied, "I am John Smith; I am a treasure hunter and explorer, and I was inspecting the wreck of the *Queen Anne's Revenge*."

"The wreck? Thou art mistaken, Master Smith; 'tis evident that the ship of which thou spokest is very much living, and ready to repair to hell and back if so commanded." As he said this, an awful smile erupted upon his face; the man knew full well that something was not right.

"I am much diverted to observe," the man continued, "that thou art not yet a part of my crew, John Smith. Thou hath owned to knowing of my fame in thy profession of my wicked name: I am indeed the pirate 'Blackbeard'…but thou shalt with much alacrity referest to me as 'Captain'…"

"I have no intention of staying," retorted Smith, whose courage began to pluck up.

"Thou hast no choice: thy event is decided upon." Blackbeard smiled again and casually produced a pistol. He laid it on the table, but his hand was not on the trigger.

The less-composed Smith swiftly parried, "Was that Maynard's thinking?" He was quickly trying to make sense of the situation and how he could best escape it. He reached for conversation bearing even the slightest ability to distract Blackbeard and put him on the defensive.

The topic was moderately successful.

"Mister Maynard cometh to all rencounters of murther with an incumbent affliction of pride," began a still-calm Blackbeard. "Such pestilence no-doubt secureth his place as author of what monster thou now beholdest...."

"...monster?"

That awful smile erupted again, and Blackbeard emitted a slow, guttural laugh. "Own thy predicament, Master Smith: thou facest a cursed shade..."

At this, the room abruptly changed again; the furnishings and intactness became eroded, while the scene outside became a chaotic mess of rain and thunder. Blackbeard himself rose, and as lightning flashed, Smith to his horror witnessed a transformation. The pirate's girth increased, with muscle tearing through once-handsome clothing: his face shot upward into that of a shark's, and his limbs became complimented with black, sharply-cut fins. He stared Smith down with white, pupil-less eyes, and spoke in a voice deeply morphed into what could only be described as 'Devil's English'.

"Seventeen-Hundred-and-Seventeen we sailed…black waters beckoned, and in the arms of the Weroansqua we invested our trust…"

The beast violently grabbed the edge of the table between him and his intruder, and effortlessly tossed it into the wall on his left; his gaze was still fixed on Smith, who was now completely lost.

"In my effort to bite death, I wast meself bitten…Malemos damned us, but I could not have known…Maynard wast my release, spoke she…"

He approached Smith as if in slow-motion, but the diver quickly reached for the door to escape. It was locked.

"Thou cannot quitest this cell, Master Smith!" roared the monster with enthusiasm. *"Thy event is dcided upon…"*

"Why?!" shouted a panicked Smith—he needed to escape—he will survive, as he's always done. "What's the point of this?! Why are you here? WHAT IS YOUR PURPOSE?!"

At this, the monster halted, bent low, and uttered so calmly, so deliberately, as if every word could break a bone, *"I have no purpose, Master Smith: I am the element with which thou elected to toy…"*

He lunged.

Smith dodged quickly to the left and towards the window—it was his only chance—he crashed through.

Instantaneously, he was back. He was right outside the ship, adjacent to the captain's quarters, in full diving gear. The weather above changed into a stormier composure, but everything else was the same…

except for…

…whispers?

Suddenly the giant Sandtiger—the Blackbeard Shark—erupted through the window that was Smith's escape. Smith immediately turned and drew his diver's knife—as the shark made a snap towards his throat, Smith dodged and stabbed it in the gills.

The combat drew attention.

The shark was wounded and faltered, giving Smith a small chance; he backpedaled to the surface and turned upward for a full ascent, focusing on his breathing and timing for fear of the bends.

But the others joined in.

Five Sandtigers circled ahead and positioned themselves between Smith and the surface. Another five approached from his right, and as Smith turned left he saw three more in the distance. The whispers were intensifying, and Smith could pick out words:

"curse…Teach…curse…Edward…"

His only option was now backwards. To his horror, the thirteen sharks followed him, lurking so orderly, so methodically, that it was absolutely unnatural. They were pressuring him towards the wreck…*they wanted him back…*

Realizing this, Smith turned to make a struggle, but he was incapacitated: two sharks immediately charged and seized his arms—they were now dragging him down…down…down towards the hatch…

The other eleven began to swarm on deck, excitedly circling…their golden skin and gleaming mouths at first shimmered, but the sky above was growing dark…

"Unforgiven are thy trespasses, John Smith"

The Blackbeard Shark swam from behind the diver and above him—its wound was completely healed. Noticing this, Smith realized that the other scars were more organized, purposeful…symbolic!

The symbols on the map!

The shark positioned itself in the center of the circle and faced the diver. The disembodied voice spoke again, but Smith now knew who it belonged to:

"As punishment, thou art now welcomed to our devoted crew…"

The whispers intensified, and the grip of Smith's captors tightened. This was the final act.

"For centuries past, we hath been…"

The swarming quickened, the mouths now smiled.

"…here to punish those who breach."

The Blackbeard Shark approached. He brought more whispers.

"And now, thou shalt…"

Closer. Tighter.

"…sufferest throughout…"

Face-to-face.

A single whisper.

"…the Curse of Edward Teach."

Respect the seas and all who call them home.

~ *Thanks* ~

photo by Van Kurt

"To my brothers, Dylan and Evan; thanks for all the love, support, and absolute hilarity. You guys are the best, and have always been the key to some of my happiest memories.

To Andy Murch, who possesses a plethora of powerful photos at Elasmodiver.com; thank you for your stunning shot of Carcharias taurus (page 21). It made all the difference.

To those who may be inspired, never trade your inspiration. You can be whomever you want; that choice is always yours. Keep improving yourself, keep practicing, and never let go of your love. "

~Zachary W. Nicholls

the First Dr. Jaws